MW01234830

JAMES
Meets the Prairie

by Katy Z. Allen

Perfection Learning® CA

About the Author

Katy Z. Allen is the coauthor of several books for children, including *Humphrey the Wrong Way Whale* and *The Great Yellowstone Fire*, both written under the name Kathryn A. Goldner. She has written numerous articles for children and adults and has written and edited many educational materials.

Katy Z. Allen is currently a storyteller, working as a team called Yad B'Yad with singer and songwriter Gabi Mezger. Together they write, perform, and record original songs and stories for children and adults of all ages.

Katy Z. Allen grew up in southeastern Wisconsin, where there was once prairie land. She now lives in Massachusetts with her two teenage sons.

Illustrations: Larry Nolte, Kay Ewald

Photo Credits: Colorado State Historical Society pp. 26, 27; Denver Public Library, Western History Department pp. 6, 8, 11, 14, 15, 17, 18, 19, 28–29, 41 top, 42, 44–45, 47 top; Carol Ewald pp. 54 top, 55 top; Iowa Department of Natural Resources, Margaret Oard pp. 36–37; Library of Congress pp. 9, 22, 23, 35; Missouri Department of Conservation page 38, back cover; Nebraska State Historical Society page 46 top; Nebraska State Historical Society, Solomon D. Butcher Collection pp. 3, 30, 31, 33 both, 34, 38, 39, 40, 41 bottom, 43, 46 bottom, 47 bottom, 48 both, cover; Oregon Historical Society page 16; Sharlot Hall Museum page 10; United States Fish and Wildlife Service pp. 17, 39; University of Oklahoma Library, Western History Collection page 32; Utah State Historical Society pp. 24, 25.

For information, contact
Perfection Learning® Corporation,
1000 North Second Avenue, P.O. Box 500,
Logan, Iowa 51546-0500
Phone: 1-800-831-4190 • Fax: 1-800-543-2745
perfectionlearning.com

Paperback ISBN 0-7891-1998-6
Cover Craft® ISBN 0-7807-6688-1

Contents

Chapter 1

An Ocean of Grass

"When will we get to the prairie, Pa?" asked James. "How much longer?"

"It won't be long now," said Pa. "Perhaps tomorrow. Maybe the day after that." Pa called to the horses and urged them on.

"I hope it is today," said James. He had heard about the prairie for weeks. He had heard about the home they would build there. And James was tired of waiting.

James listened to the wind in the tall trees that lined the wagon trail. There were so many trees. He could not see beyond them.

James was glad he was riding up front. He felt sorry for his sisters, Faith and Beth. They were riding in the back of the wagon with Ma. They could only look behind. They only saw where they had been.

The wagon rumbled on. James thought about his old home near the ocean. He missed the sound of the pounding waves.

Then James remembered the prairie. He thought about his aunt and uncle. He thought about how his family would build a new home near them. He grew excited. Soon he forgot about the ocean.

James saw sunlight through the trees. "The prairie!" he thought.

James stood up to see better. No, he was wrong. It was just a clearing. A farm stood in the center of the clearing. Sadly, James sat down again.

The wagon rolled past the clearing. James and his father saw a boy with a dog. The two walked toward the farm. James and his father waved.

The boy reminded James of his friend Will. He remembered digging clams with Will. He remembered building sand castles together.

James missed his friend. "What is Will doing now?" he wondered.

James kept looking ahead. He wanted to get to the prairie. "The trees look smaller," he said to his father. "And they look farther apart."

"You're right. They do," said Pa. "We must be near the prairie."

Still the wagon rumbled on. Again James saw light through the trees. He held his breath.

Suddenly, the wagon left the forest.

"The prairie!" cried James. "We are here!"

James could not believe his eyes. The sky was as big here as it was over the ocean. "Maybe bigger," James said to himself. Ahead, the prairie stretched as far as James could see.

"It looks like the ocean!" said James. Tall grasses and flowers waved in the wind. The wagon seemed like a ship riding ocean waves. James was happy. "I feel at home here," he said.

Chapter 2

Swish! Buzz! Chirp!

Within minutes, they left the forest behind. "I want to see the prairie up close," said James.

He climbed down from the wagon and raced ahead. The grasses were so high! They were over his head.

"Don't get lost," warned Pa.

"I won't," answered James.

"How could anyone get lost here? The prairie is so open," James thought.

James ran on. Soon he could not hear the wind in the trees.

James only heard the swish of the grasses. He heard the plants bumping into each other.

James turned off the trail. Tall plants rose all around him. He could see only a few feet ahead.

Everywhere he turned he saw green
grass. He saw orange and yellow flowers
and pink and red flowers. He saw white
and blue flowers. Butterflies rested on
many of them.

Grasshoppers jumped. A bee flew by James. Bzzzz, bzzzz, bzzzz. A mosquito buzzed in his ear. He slapped at it and missed.

James heard loud chirping. He looked up. Birds filled the blue sky.

James looked toward the trail. But he couldn't see it. He could see only plants and insects.

Now James understood what Pa had meant. He knew how he could get lost in the prairie.

James hurried back toward the trail. He was happy to see the wagon and his family.

Chapter 3

A Prairie Town

The days passed. The family traveled westward. The prairie grasses were shorter.

One day, James heard a strange sound. "Pa, do you hear barking?" James asked.

"I hear something," his father answered.

Suddenly, James noticed small animals nibbling on the grass. The grass was very, very short.

"Look!" cried James. "Little dogs!"

When he called out, the small animals jumped. Then they were gone.

"Prairie dogs," said Pa. "But they aren't really dogs. They belong to the squirrel family. They are afraid of us. So they went down into their burrows. There they are safe."

Pa stopped the horses. He and James climbed down. Beth, Faith, and Ma joined them.

Everywhere, the ground was covered with huge holes. The family stood quietly by the wagon.

Before long, the little animals returned. They no longer seemed scared.

Some prairie dogs chewed on grass. Others tumbled about. Some dug at their burrows. They threw dirt behind them.

Near one hole, some young prairie dogs lined up like soldiers. All stood on their hind legs. An adult prairie dog stood beside them. The adult barked. Then the little ones tried to bark.

James and his sisters laughed. "It's a school for barking," said Faith.

A silent hawk floated high in the sky. Its shadow fell on the land. James heard many loud barks. The prairie dogs scurried in all directions. Again, they were gone.

"They will stay down longer this time," explained Pa. "The hawk is a real danger."

A rattle sounded nearby. "A rattlesnake!" cried Ma. "There!" She pointed toward a hole.

"Into the wagon!" shouted Pa.

The snake slipped into the hole. The family hurried into the wagon. Pa clucked to the horses. Quickly, they left the prairie dog town behind.

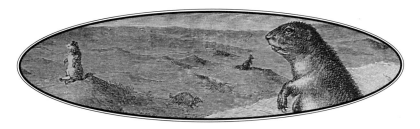

Chapter 4

Thunder!

James leaned back and looked at the sky. He pretended he was a bird. He saw himself swoop and glide.

The wagon jerked and stopped. James sat up. He noticed that the plants looked different.

"What happened?" James asked.

"The wagon is stuck," said Pa. "The ground is wet. Everyone out."

They all climbed down. The horses pulled hard. Everyone pushed. Slowly, slowly, the wagon moved ahead.

The wet area ended. So they climbed back onto the wagon. James sat in the back with his sisters. Ma sat up front with Pa.

James looked behind. He saw hundreds of ducks and geese. Some flew on. Others landed nearby.

"Look," James said to his sisters. "There's a pond over there."

"A thousand birds must live there," said Faith.

"Maybe a million," said Beth.

James looked up at the sky. "It's getting cloudy. Maybe there will be a storm."

Faith shivered. "I hope not," she said.

The wagon continued westward. The pond passed from sight.

James was tired of the trip. He wished it would end. He wanted to see his aunt and uncle. He wanted to help build a new home.

James leaned lazily against the wagon. He watched tiny hummingbirds. They buzzed from flower to flower like bees.

Suddenly, James heard a distant rumble. "Thunder," he told his sisters. "A storm is coming."

Again the wagon halted. James saw his father studying some plants. The plants were ten feet high and had big yellow flowers. "What are you looking at, Pa?" he asked.

"Compass plants," said Pa. "See, their leaves point north. That means we are still headed west."

The sky darkened. The wind whipped faster. The prairie grasses bent low.

"The storm is coming from the west," observed James.

"Yes," said Pa. "There's no shelter nearby. We'll have to stay here. We're in a low spot. We'll be safe."

Pa turned the horses. Now they faced
out of the wind. He checked the wagon.
Everything was fastened.

The whole family crawled under the wagon. They were just in time. Rain began to pound the prairie.

Lightning flashed. Thunder clapped like cannon shots. Wind whipped the canvas of the wagon. It flapped loudly.

The horses whinnied. Faith cried out in fear. Ma held her close.

Everyone huddled together. Rain poured from the sky.

As fast as it began, the storm ended. The sun shone. James and the others crawled out.

The air smelled of earth. Water dripped from the grasses.

"Everything smells new and fresh," said Ma. They all agreed.

5

Chapter

Bison, Bison, and More Bison

James rode in the back of the wagon.
He thought he heard thunder again. He
looked up. The sky was clear and blue.

How could there be another storm?

Suddenly the wagon stopped again. James and his sisters jumped down. They rushed to the front of the wagon.

"Look at that!" cried James.

"What are they?" asked Beth.

"There are so many!" said Faith.

"A herd of bison," said Pa. "They are going north. We cannot get by them. We will have to wait until they pass."

Everyone climbed into the front of the wagon. They watched in silence. The bison headed north. They made a big cloud of dust.

"The Indians hunt bison," explained Pa. "They use them for everything."

"They are so big!" said Beth.

"Huge!" said Faith.

"The Indians eat the meat," Pa went on. "They even use the hide. They use it to build their homes. They even make clothes from it."

Ma opened a food box. She gave chunks of bread to James and the others. "We might as well eat our lunch," she said. "We'll be here a long time."

Pa agreed. "It's too bad," he said. "We're near the end of our trip."

"When will we get there?" asked Faith.

"Tomorrow or the next day," answered Pa.

James jumped for joy. "Yippee! No more wagon ride!"

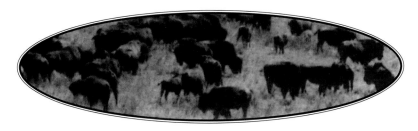

Chapter 6

A New Home

Pa reined in the horses. They stopped beside a low sod home. A woman stood at the door. She wiped her hands on her apron, then waved. A man and two boys came running from the barn.

James and his sisters tumbled from the wagon. The families rushed toward each other. They hugged and kissed.

"Welcome, welcome," said Aunt Sarah, over and over. "Thank goodness you arrived safely."

Aunt Sarah served them cold milk and cookies. James had not had a cookie for months. Had they always tasted so good?

"Thomas, I can't wait," said Pa. "I know we just arrived. Still, I want to see our land. I want to see where our new home will be."

"I thought you might," said Uncle Thomas. He stood up. "I'll show you."

"I want to see it too!" James said, jumping to his feet.

"Me too," said Faith.

Beth and Ma stood up. "We'll all go," said Ma.

"Come along then," said Uncle Thomas.

James and his family followed Uncle Thomas. The cousins and Aunt Sarah went too.

They walked past the barn and along a fence line. To James, it seemed as if they walked for miles.

At last, Uncle Thomas stopped. He spread out his arms. "This is your land," he said.

James stared in silence. Then he rushed ahead. He ran down a small hill.

There, trees lined a small stream.

"Trees!" he cried. "And water too!"

James climbed one of the trees. He climbed to the very top.

James saw other farms off in the distance. Mostly, he saw prairie in all directions.

James waved to the others. "Land ahoy!" he cried. "I see a new land!"

"My new home," James said to himself. He liked what he saw. "I think I'll be very happy here."

7

Chapter

The Prairie

A prairie is a kind of land. The land is flat. But there are a few small hills.

Rivers, streams, and lakes provide water on the prairie. Special plants grow there. Special animals live there.

Tall grass once grew on the prairie. The grass grew taller than most people. Some people even got lost in it. There weren't many trees.

Early travelers saw many animals on the prairie. Prairie dogs were a common sight. They got their name because they barked like dogs.

Rattlesnakes also lived on the prairie. Their bites made people sick. People wore tall boots so the snakes couldn't bite them.

Bison roamed the prairie. They were
very important to the Native Americans.
The Native Americans hunted bison and
ate the meat.

Bison fur is soft and warm. Native
Americans made clothes from the fur.

They made tools from the bones. They
even used the stomach to make cooking
pots!

Many plants grew on the prairie.
There were grasses of green and gold
and flowers of many colors.

There was also clover. Bees made honey from clover. Since there wasn't any sugar on the prairie, honey was a sweet treat!

Special plants like the compass plant helped the people on the prairie. This tall plant had yellow flowers. Its leaves pointed north and south. Travelers looked at the plant to make sure they were going the right way.

Chapter 8

The Pioneers

People from the East traveled to the prairie to find land for new homes. They were called *pioneers.* They rode in wagons. The trip took weeks. Sometimes the trip took months.

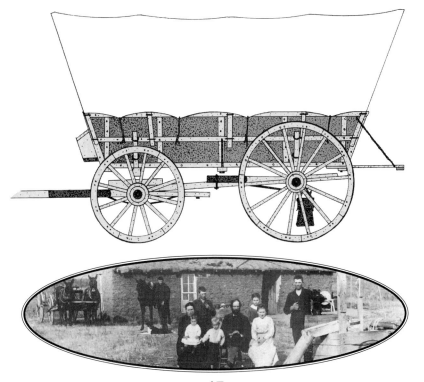

Horses and oxen pulled the heavy wagons. The wagons had roofs made of canvas. The pioneers often used the wagons for shelter.

The wagons were full of clothes and food. There were boxes of seeds and tools. Some families brought chickens and cows.

The people brought everything they needed. There were no supermarkets on the prairie!

One person drove the wagon. Others rode inside. Sometimes people walked. They had to stay on the trail. It was easy to get lost on the prairie.

Sometimes several families traveled together. They traveled in a single line. This was called a *wagon train.*

The wagons had to cross streams and rivers. But there weren't any bridges. So everyone got out of the wagons. The drivers led the horses and oxen across. They waded across the stream or river.

Sometimes one family went west first. They settled the land. They sent word back east to family and friends. Then other families came. The families helped each other. There was enough work for everyone.

The pioneers built their own houses.
There weren't any boards or bricks.
So pioneers built houses from dirt
called sod.

The sod was cut into blocks. Pioneers built walls and a roof from sod. They made the door from boards. These boards usually came from the wagon.

The sod house was dark. It was like a cave. But it was warm and dry.

The pioneers built farms on the prairie. They grew wheat and corn. They raised cows and pigs. They made their own butter and cheese.

Some people raised sheep. They made clothes from the wool. Today people still farm where there was once prairie.

Greenland

North America

Atlantic Ocean

Pacific Ocean

N

South America

Major grasslands
of the world

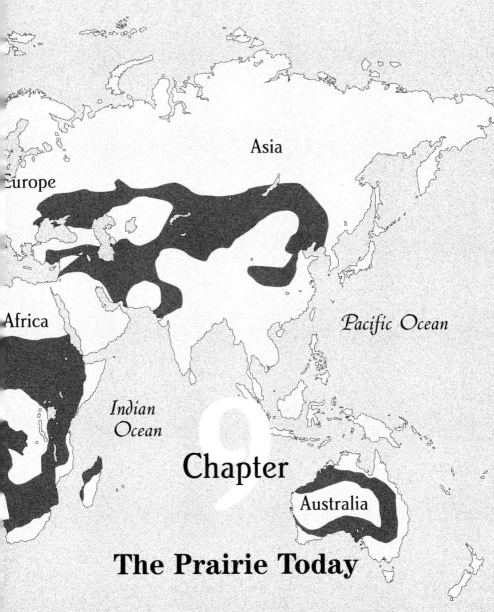

Chapter 9

The Prairie Today

Prairies are found all over the world.
In Russia, the prairies are called *steppes*.
In Africa, they are called *savannas*. The
pampas is the prairie in Argentina.

53

Prairies in the United States once covered Iowa, Indiana, and Illinois. They were also found in Nebraska, Kansas, and other central states.

The prairie doesn't look the same as it did in the days of the pioneers. A few prairie dogs and bison still live on the prairie. Most live in national parks or zoos.

Prairie plants are not common anymore. Some people are trying to reclaim the prairie. They plant special areas with prairie flowers and grasses.

There are many farms on the prairie now. There are also towns and cities. Omaha was once a prairie town. It grew into a major city. Kansas City and Chicago grew the same way.

Do you live where prairie grass and bison once lived?

Look for these other Cover-to-Cover chapter books!

The Elephant's Ancestors

Great Eagle and Small One

The Jesse Owens Story

Little Fish

Magic Tricks and More

What If You'd Been at Jamestown?

What's New with Mr. Pizooti?

The Whooping Crane

Yankee Doodle and the Secret Society

21st CCLC

Tigers Den After-School Academy

Northwest Elementary